WONDER

解讀攻略

戴逸群 —— 編著

Joseph E. Schier —— 審閱

三民書局

國家圖書館出版品預行編目資料

Wonder 解讀攻略／戴逸群編著.－－初版一刷.－－
臺北市：三民，2020
　　面；　　公分.－－（閱讀成癮）

　ISBN 978–957–14–6809–9　（平裝）
　1. 英語 2. 讀本

805.18　　　　　　　　　　　　　　109004847

閱讀成癮

Wonder 解讀攻略

編 著 者	戴逸群
審　　閱	Joseph E. Schier
責任編輯	楊雅雯
美術編輯	王立涵
內頁繪圖	Steph Pai
封面繪圖	Steph Pai

發 行 人	劉振強
出 版 者	三民書局股份有限公司
地　　址	臺北市復興北路 386 號 (復北門市)
	臺北市重慶南路一段 61 號 (重南門市)
電　　話	(02)25006600
網　　址	三民網路書店 https://www.sanmin.com.tw

出版日期	初版一刷 2020 年 5 月
書籍編號	S870460
I S B N	978-957-14-6809-9

三民書局

——— 序 ———

　　新課綱強調以「學生」為中心的教與學，注重學生的學習動機與熱情。而英文科首重語言溝通、互動的功能性，培養學生「自主學習」與「終身學習」的能力與習慣。小說「解讀攻略」就是因應新課綱的精神，在「英文小說中毒團隊」的努力下孕育而生。

　　一系列的「解讀攻略」旨在引導學生能透過原文小說的閱讀學習獨立思考，運用所學的知識與技能解決問題；此外也藉由廣泛閱讀進行跨文化反思，提升社會參與並培養國際觀。

　　「英文小說中毒團隊」由普高技高英文老師與大學教授組成，嚴選出主題多樣豐富、適合英文學習的原文小說。我們從文本延伸，設計多元有趣的閱讀素養活動，培養學生從讀懂文本到表達所思的英文能力。團隊秉持著改變臺灣英文教育的使命感，期許我們的努力能為臺灣的英文教育注入一股活水，翻轉大家對英文學習的想像！

戴逸群

Contents

Picture Credits

All pictures in this publication are authorized for use by Steph Pai and Shutterstock.

1

Part One: August
Pages 1–16

Word Power

1. crack up 哈哈大笑
2. cleft palate *n.* 唇顎裂
3. duel *v.* 決鬥
4. fraction *n.* 分數
5. drool *v.* 流口水
6. rearview mirror *n.* 後照鏡
7. blind date *n.* 相親
8. elective *n.* 選修課

Reading Comprehension

( ) 1. Why was Auggie homeschooled until he was ten?
    (A) Because of the way he looked.
    (B) Because of all the surgeries he had.
    (C) Because no school was willing to accept him.
    (D) Because his sister didn't allow him to go to school.

( ) 2. Why does Auggie's mother think fifth grade is a better time for Auggie to start school?
    (A) Fifth grade is not only the first year of middle school but also a brand-new start for every kid, including Auggie.
    (B) Their family finally saved enough money to send him to private school.
    (C) The subjects in fifth grade are so important that Auggie can't miss them.
    (D) His mother wants to go back to work and can't homeschool him anymore.

( ) 3. What does Mr. Tushman have in store for Auggie?
    (A) A Halloween parade.
    (B) A science fair.
    (C) An Egyptian Museum exhibit.
    (D) A school tour.

Further Discussion

1. How does Via see Auggie in the "Ordinary" chapter? Does she see Auggie as an ordinary kid? Why or why not?

_____

_____

_____

_____

_____

_____

2. While driving back home, Auggie's parents have different opinions about sending Auggie to middle school. If you were Auggie's parent, would you send him to school? Why or why not?

_____

_____

_____

_____

_____

_____

3. Find more descriptions about Mr. Tushman in the book. What do we know about him? Try to describe this character in terms of his job, appearance, and personality.

_____

_____

_____

_____

_____

Character Log

Find and write down each character's basic information, physical appearance or personality traits from pages 1 to 34, and draw a picture of each character.

August (also Auggie)

· ten-year-old kid
· *Star Wars* fan
· ordinary vs. extraordinary

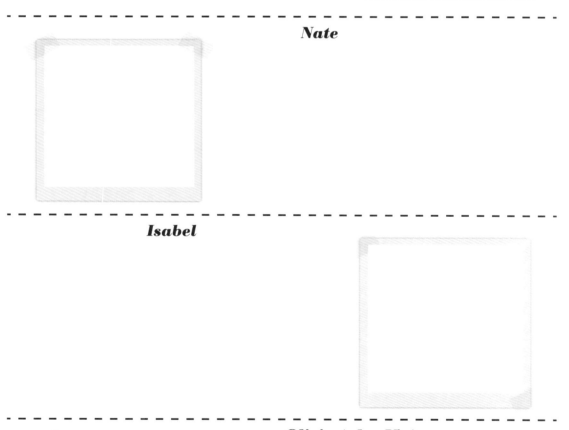

Nate

Isabel

Olivia (also Via)

Mr. Tushman

- -

Jack Will

- -

Julian

- -

Charlotte

2

Part One: August
Pages 17–34

Word Power

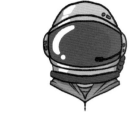

1. combination *n.* 密碼鎖
2. bangs *n.* 瀏海
3. incubator *n.* 孵化器
4. Bunsen burner *n.* 本生燈
5. mumble *v.* 含糊地說
6. smirk *n.* 得意的笑
7. dork *n.* 笨蛋
8. obnoxious *adj.* 令人討厭的

Reading Comprehension

( ) 1. Who is Auggie's homeroom teacher?
    (A) Mr. Browne.
    (B) Mrs. Garcia.
    (C) Ms. Petosa.
    (D) Mr. Haller.

( ) 2. Who played the leading role in the play *Oliver*?
    (A) Jack.
    (B) Charlotte.
    (C) Julian.
    (D) Via.

( ) 3. What hint does Auggie give his mother to show that he wants to leave the school?
    (A) Feeding Daisy.
    (B) Picking Via up.
    (C) Playing ball with Christopher.
    (D) Going to the doctor.

Further Discussion

1. Who is Mr. T and what's his famous catchphrase? Use the Internet to find out the answer.

   _____

   _____

   _____

   _____

   _____

   _____

2. Julian asks about Auggie's face rudely by asking "What's the deal with your face?" In your opinion, what would be more polite expressions to use regarding this subject?

   _____

   _____

   _____

   _____

   _____

   _____

3. Mr. Tushman asks Julian, Jack Will and Charlotte to take Auggie on a little tour of the school. If you were Auggie, whom would you like to be friends with after the grand tour? Why would you choose him/her as your friend?

   _____

   _____

   _____

   _____

   _____

   _____

 **Character Image**

Find a quote from each character and tell us about your first impression about him/her.

Character's Quote

Character's Image

Character's Quote	Character's Image
# Mr. Tushman "No one calls me Mr. T. Though I have a feeling I'm called a lot of other things I don't know about. Let's face it, a name like mine is not so easy to live with, you know what I mean?"	He is understanding and empathetic.
# Charlotte	
# Julian	
# Jack Will	

3

Part One: August
Pages 35–53

 Word Power

1. butterflies in sb's stomach 很緊張
2. take attendance 點名
3. curse *v.* 罵髒話
4. scrunch up sb's face 揉某人的臉
5. braid *n.* 辮子
6. doodle *v.* 塗鴉
7. precept *n.* 箴言
8. cool beans 酷斃了

 Reading Comprehension

( ) 1. How does Auggie feel on his first day of school?
    (A) Excited.
    (B) Bored.
    (C) Nervous.
    (D) Joyful.

( ) 2. What is Mr. Browne's September precept?
    (A) When given the choice between being right or being kind, choose kind.
    (B) Your deeds are your monuments.
    (C) Have no friends not equal to yourself.
    (D) No man is an island, entire of itself.

( ) 3. Which of the following is **NOT** true about Auggie when he first goes to the lunchroom?
    (A) People stare at him and nudge each other.
    (B) People watch him out of the corners of their eyes.
    (C) Jack is sitting on Auggie's side of the room.
    (D) No one saves a seat for him.

Further Discussion

1. A metaphor is an imaginative expression that can make a story more vivid. For example, Isabel refers to Via's birth as "a walk in the park." This metaphor indicates Via's birth was an easy task. Read the chapter "Locks" and explain the metaphorical meaning of "locks."

_____
_____
_____
_____
_____
_____

2. In the "Lamb to the Slaughter" chapter, why does Julian mention Darth Sidious to Auggie?

_____
_____
_____
_____
_____
_____

3. There is a connection between August and Summer—their name theme. Try to think of a name theme related to your English name and come up with some names belonging to this theme.

_____
_____
_____
_____
_____
_____

Julian's Diary

Imagine yourself as Julian and record the day when you gave Auggie a tour of the school in your diary. Try to find the details in the book and express your thoughts and feelings. Remember to use the past tense.

4

Part One: August
Pages 54-67

Word Power

1. snuggle *v.* 依偎
2. tuck sb in 幫某人蓋被子
3. good call 好決定
4. never a dull moment 絕無冷場

5. contagious *adj.* 會傳染的
6. pimple *n.* 青春痘
7. teensy-weensy *adj.* 極小的
8. RSVP 敬請回覆

Reading Comprehension

( ) 1. How long does it take the entire school to get used to Auggie's face?
    (A) One week.
    (B) Two weeks.
    (C) One month.
    (D) Two years.

( ) 2. What does Jack think Auggie should do when people stare at him?
    (A) He should pinch them in the face.
    (B) He should squirt them in the face.
    (C) He should elbow them.
    (D) He should smile at them.

( ) 3. Whose mother doesn't reply to Auggie's party invitation?
    (A) Charlotte's mother.
    (B) Jack's mother.
    (C) Henry's mother.
    (D) Julian's mother.

Further Discussion

1. When Auggie talks about Summer, why does he use a simile to compare himself and Summer to *Beauty and the Beast*?

_____

_____

_____

_____

_____

_____

2. Read the chapter "Wake Me Up when September Ends." Why does Auggie mention "a Wookiee" in this chapter?

_____

_____

_____

_____

_____

_____

3. Why does Isabel say "The apple doesn't fall far from the tree"? What does this proverb mean?

_____

_____

_____

_____

_____

_____

 ## Your Own Motto

People might take old proverbs, quotes from books, song lyrics or famous lines from movies as their mottos. Find one for yourself and state the reason why you chose it. Then, create a logo on the T-shirt.

Here are some examples:

Stay hungry. Stay foolish. —Steve Jobs

The biggest adventure you can take is to live the life of your dreams. —Oprah Winfrey

I don't dream at night, I dream at day, I dream all day; I'm dreaming for living.
—Steven Spielberg

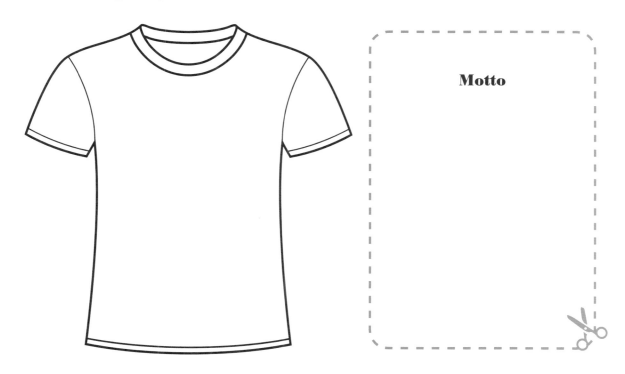

Motto

5

Part One: August
Pages 68–80

Word Power

1. politically correct *adj.* 政治正確的
2. squint *v.* 瞇著眼看
3. dorky *adj.* 蠢的
4. phobia *n.* 恐懼症

5. aversion *n.* 厭惡
6. make a face 做鬼臉
7. ditch *v.* 擺脫，拋棄
8. run a temperature 發燒

Reading Comprehension

(　) 1. What did Summer really want to be for Halloween?
    (A) A Goth girl.
    (B) Hermione.
    (C) The Wicked Witch of the West.
    (D) A unicorn.

(　) 2. In which classes does Auggie notice that people avoid touching him?
    (A) Math and English.
    (B) History and Geography.
    (C) PE and Art.
    (D) Dance and Science.

(　) 3. What does Auggie dress up as for Halloween this year?
    (A) Boba Fett.
    (B) Clone Trooper.
    (C) Bleeding Scream.
    (D) Obi-Wan Kenobi.

Further Discussion

1. Why did Summer intend to prepare two different costumes for Halloween?

_____
_____
_____
_____
_____
_____

2. Which holiday does Auggie prefer, Halloween or Christmas? What are the differences between Auggie as himself and as Bleeding Scream at school?

_____
_____
_____
_____
_____
_____

3. What might be the reason that Julian changed his mind and dressed up as Darth Sidious on Halloween?

_____
_____
_____
_____
_____
_____

Your Halloween Costume

Halloween is a holiday when people put on costumes and go trick-or-treating. What is your favorite costume for Halloween? Please draw your favorite character and tell us why. The following are some costume ideas for you to consider.

Classics	witch, wizard, ghost, mummy, devil, pirate, werewolf, vampire, princess, etc.
Harry Potter	Harry, Ron, Hermione, Snape, Voldemort, Dumbledore, etc.
Fictional Characters	Frankenstein, Catwoman, Superman, Wonder Woman, Captain Marvel, Batman, Iron Man, Spider Man, etc.
Disney Characters	Elsa, Belle, Ariel, Aladdin, Sulley, Woody, Hulk, Peter Pan, etc.
Fantasy Animals	unicorn, dragon, Bigfoot, My Little Pony, etc.
Video Game Characters	Super Mario Brothers, Zelda, Pokémon characters, Sonic the Hedgehog, Street Fighter characters, etc.

My favorite costume for Halloween is . . . .

6

Part Two: Via
Pages 81–102

Word Power

1. cramp *n.* 經痛 (常用複數 cramps)
2. hipster *n.* 文青，潮人
3. fashionista *n.* 時尚教主
4. out of the blue 出乎意料地

5. brainy *n.* 學霸
6. jock *n.* 體育迷
7. a lump in sb's throat 某人哽咽
8. let sb off the hook 放某人一馬

Reading Comprehension

( ) 1. What role does Auggie play in his family's galaxy?
    (A) Planet.
    (B) Comet.
    (C) Sun.
    (D) Asteroid.

( ) 2. What did Grans die of?
    (A) The flu.
    (B) A heart attack.
    (C) Lung cancer.
    (D) Severe head injuries.

( ) 3. What didn't Miranda do with Auggie?
    (A) Sing "Space Oddity" with him.
    (B) Talk to him about *Avatar*.
    (C) Hug him and play with him.
    (D) Go camping with him.

Further Discussion

1. In the "A Tour of the Galaxy" chapter, do you think Via was jealous of all the attention Auggie got? Why or why not?

_____
_____
_____
_____
_____
_____

2. How did Via feel when she was with Miranda and Ella in middle school? What are the differences between the ways they get along with each other in middle school and high school?

_____
_____
_____
_____
_____
_____

3. Why did Via get mad when she found out Auggie had cut off his braid?

_____
_____
_____
_____
_____
_____

Music Appreciation—"Space Oddity"

Have you ever heard this song before? Listen to the song and think about the following questions. Then write down your answers.

David Bowie — "Space Oddity"

1. What is the song about, and what does it try to convey?

2. Why does the author start Via's part by quoting the lyrics from the song?

3. When might people want to listen to a song like "Space Oddity"?

7

Part Two: Via
Pages 103–117

Word Power

1. genetics 101 *n.* 遺傳學入門
2. like two peas in a pod 一個模子刻出來
3. Polaroid *n.* 拍立得照片
4. mutant gene *n.* 突變基因
5. tic-tac-toe *n.* 井字遊戲
6. make a clean break 劃清界線
7. at the top of sb's lung 某人聲嘶力竭
8. have a stomach bug 肚子痛

Reading Comprehension

( ) 1. Which of the following countries is **NOT** included in the exotic mix of the Pullman family gene pool?
(A) Poland.   (B) Brazil.
(C) Italy.   (D) Russia.

( ) 2. Where did Via meet Eleanor for the first time?
(A) At PS22.
(B) At a party.
(C) At a camp.
(D) In high school.

( ) 3. Why is Halloween a sad time of year for Via and her mom?
(A) They have to go trick-or-treating with Auggie.
(B) It is around the time Grans died.
(C) They have to make costumes for Auggie.
(D) They have to prepare a big family dinner.

Further Discussion

1. What's wrong with the friendship between Miranda and Via in high school?

_____
_____
_____
_____
_____
_____

2. If you were Isabel, what would you do to balance your role of Auggie's mom and that of Via's mom?

_____
_____
_____
_____
_____
_____

3. How did Via persuade Auggie to go back to school after learning about Jack's betrayal of Auggie?

_____
_____
_____
_____
_____
_____

Via's Emotional Range

The following are six events that Via has experienced. Try to draw Via's emotional range and describe her feelings during the events.

Happy

Sad

| Staying with Grans in Montauk for four weeks | Hearing the news about Grans' death | Middle school time with Miranda and Ella | Seeing Miranda on the first day of school | Learning that Auggie had cut off his Padawan braid | Hearing Auggie say that Miranda missed her |

Events	Via's feelings
Staying with Grans in Montauk for four weeks (p. 85)	It was an amazing, happy, and carefree period of time for Via because she could be free of all the stuff that made her mad.
Hearing the news about Grans' death	
Middle school time with Miranda and Ella	
Seeing Miranda on the first day of school	
Learning that Auggie had cut off his Padawan braid	
Hearing Auggie say that Miranda missed her	

8

Part Three: Summer
Pages 118–132

 Word Power

1. plague *n.* 瘟疫
2. hang out 鬼混
3. hand sanitizer *n.* 乾洗手
4. That's a bummer. 真掃興

5. vibe *n.* 氛圍
6. pinky swear *v.* 打勾勾
7. Rated R 限制級 (電影)
8. biracial *adj.* 雙種族的

 Reading Comprehension

(　) 1. What cruel game have the kids been playing since the beginning of the year?
    (A) The Plague.
    (B) Hopscotch.
    (C) Four Square.
    (D) Musical Chairs.

(　) 2. Why did Auggie act weird in front of Summer after Halloween?
    (A) He thought that Summer was pretending to be friends with him.
    (B) He had a crush on Summer.
    (C) He once heard Summer bad-mouthing him.
    (D) He wanted to be friends with Jack instead of Summer.

(　) 3. What kind of Egyptian costumes did **NOT** appear at the exhibit?
    (A) Archaeologist.
    (B) Pharaoh.
    (C) Sphinx.
    (D) Mummy.

Further Discussion

1. How did Summer see Auggie at first? And how did Summer see Auggie after getting along with him?

_____
_____
_____
_____
_____
_____

2. Why did Summer mention there were no unicorns at the Halloween Parade?

_____
_____
_____
_____
_____
_____

3. Why is the chapter called "Warning: This Kid Is Rated R"? How does it connect to Summer's warning to her mother?

_____
_____
_____
_____
_____
_____

Music Appreciation—"This Is Me"

Have you heard this song before? Try to think about the following questions when you listen to the song. Then write down your answers.

🎬 The Greatest Showman — "This Is Me"

1. What does the song try to convey?

2. In *Wonder*, who do you think might love the song? What impact may the song have on him/her?

3. If you need to choose one song to best describe you, what song would you choose? Why?

9

Part Four: Jack
Pages 133-154

Word Power

1. flattering *adj.* 奉承的
2. phony *n.* 偽君子
3. goody two-shoes *n.* 乖乖牌
4. rise to the occasion 成功應對困難
5. dis *v.* 無禮對待
6. sled *n.* 雪橇
7. hobo *n.* 遊民
8. puke *v.* 嘔吐

Reading Comprehension

(　) 1. Where did Jack first see Auggie?
  (A) At the Carvel.
  (B) At the Baskin-Robbins.
  (C) At the Cold Stone Creamery.
  (D) At the Häagen-Dazs.

(　) 2. Why did Jack agree to Mr. Tushman's request for helping Auggie out?
  (A) He wanted to protect Auggie from Julian's bullying.
  (B) His mom insisted that he should do so.
  (C) He knew Auggie would be teased at school.
  (D) He was not willing to hear his mother's lecture.

(　) 3. What is "Lightning"?
  (A) Jack's armor.
  (B) Auggie's lightsaber.
  (C) Jack's sled.
  (D) Auggie's blaster.

Further Discussion

1. If your best friend found out you had spoken ill of him/her behind his/her back, what would you do?

_____

_____

_____

_____

_____

_____

2. Give an example of "Sometimes you don't have to mean to hurt someone to hurt him/her." How can you prevent situations like these from happening?

_____

_____

_____

_____

_____

_____

3. How did Jack feel about not being Auggie's friend? Try to answer by listing pros and cons.

_____

_____

_____

_____

_____

_____

Music Enthusiast

Find a song to represent each character and tell us why.

Song / Singer	Character	The Reason Why You Chose It
▶ Beautiful by Christina Aguilera	Auggie	Beauty isn't defined by other people. Auggie is beautiful no matter what they say, and words can't bring him down.

Part Four: Jack
Pages 155-174

Word Power

1. baby tooth *n.* 乳牙
2. expulsion *n.* 退學
3. clean slate *n.* 既往不咎
4. suspend *v.* 暫令停學

5. warrant *v.* 使有必要
6. on the fringe of 在…的邊緣
7. inside scoop *n.* 內幕消息
8. pout *v.* 噘嘴

Reading Comprehension

( ) 1. Why didn't Jack explain his behavior to Mr. Tushman?
  (A) Because he also bad-mouthed Auggie.
  (B) Because he was afraid of being bullied by Julian.
  (C) Because he wanted to maintain his friendship with Julian.
  (D) Because he was afraid of being expelled from school.

( ) 2. What did Julian's mom imply in her e-mail?
  (A) Auggie has emotional problems.
  (B) Auggie is disabled and is not qualified to enter the school.
  (C) Auggie has unexpectedly violent behavior.
  (D) Auggie is from an underprivileged family.

( ) 3. What happened to Jack at school after winter break?
  (A) He was welcomed by his classmates.
  (B) He was isolated by his classmates.
  (C) He was punched by Julian.
  (D) He finally got the chance to join the popular group.

Further Discussion

1. Compare the two families' holiday cards in the "Season's Greetings" chapter. What differences do you see between the two families?

   _____
   _____
   _____
   _____
   _____
   _____

2. What do you think about Mr. Tushman's response to Melissa Albans's e-mail? Do you agree with his statement? Why or why not?

   _____
   _____
   _____
   _____
   _____
   _____
   _____

3. From Charlotte's inside scoop, how did Julian convince others to take his side in the war?

   _____
   _____
   _____
   _____
   _____
   _____

The following is Jack's post on social media. Assuming that you are one of his friends or family members, what would be your comment on his post?

	Jackalope Will	Dec 31 at 5:40 PM

Jackalope Will   Dec 31 at 5:40 PM

I'm so glad we'r frenz agen ✌ —with **Auggie Doggie Pullman**

👍 Like   💬 Comment   ➦ Share

Information

♥ Relationship

_____

🎒 Hometown

_____

🏠 School

_____

Friends

_____
_____
_____
_____

Family

_____
_____
_____

Auggie Doggie Pullman

Summer Dawson

Charlotte Cody

Amanda Will

11

Part Four: Jack
Pages 175–185

Word Power

1. hypocrite *n.* 偽君子
2. chill *v.* 鬼混
3. air quotes *n.* 空氣引號
4. run errands 出門辦事
5. science-fair project *n.* 科展作品
6. spud *n.* 馬鈴薯
7. mischievously *adv.* 淘氣地
8. mess with sb 招惹某人

Reading Comprehension

(　) 1. What does Auggie **NOT** have in his room?
    (A) An Xbox 360.
    (B) A huge poster of *The Empire Strikes Back*.
    (C) A NASA flag.
    (D) *Star Wars* miniatures.

(　) 2. What do Jack and August choose for their science-fair project?
    (A) Making a volcano.
    (B) Making a pinhole camera.
    (C) Creating a potato battery.
    (D) Making crystal spikes out of Epsom salt.

(　) 3. What does Jack guess Justin is carrying?
    (A) A fiddle.
    (B) A machine gun.
    (C) A zydeco instrument.
    (D) A lightsaber.

 **Further Discussion**

1. Why did Auggie smile and say, "Welcome to my world"?

_____

_____

_____

_____

_____

_____

2. The students are divided into several kinds of groups in Auggie's school. In your school, what kinds of groups are the students divided into? Which group do you belong to?

_____

_____

_____

_____

_____

_____

3. After you read the story from Jack's point of view, why do you think the author starts Jack's part by taking a quote from _The Little Prince_?

_____

_____

_____

_____

_____

_____

OREO Opinion

When you are writing a persuasive paragraph, the OREO method is a good way to state your opinion. Do you think Jack Will is a brave kid with a sense of justice? Use the OREO method to tell us your opinion.

Opinion	Write a topic sentence to state your opinion.
Reason	Tell us why you think that way.
Examples	Give one to three examples as textual evidence and connect the examples with your reason.
Opinion	Restate your opinion in other words.

12

Part Five: Justin
Pages 186–204

 Word Power

1. freak out 嚇壞了
2. floppy disk *n.* 磁碟片
3. circuit board *n.* 電路板
4. understudy *n.* 候補演員，替身

5. audition *n.* 試鏡
6. grit sb's teeth 某人咬牙切齒
7. varsity *n.* 校隊
8. periodic table *n.* 週期表

 Reading Comprehension

(　) 1. What does Via want to be in the future?
    (A) A musician.
    (B) A geneticist.
    (C) An illustrator.
    (D) An actress.

(　) 2. Who plays Emily Gibbs in the play *Our Town*?
    (A) Charlotte.
    (B) Ella.
    (C) Miranda.
    (D) Via.

(　) 3. What does Justin compare Via to when she's fragile?
    (A) A lost bird looking for its nest.
    (B) A ladybug crawling on a leaf.
    (C) A firefly flying in the sky.
    (D) A rose withering in the desert.

Further Discussion

1. What is Justin's family like? How does Justin feel about his family?

_____

_____

_____

_____

_____

_____

2. Via and Justin made a wish on a ladybug, hoping to attract good luck. What other things bring people good luck other than ladybugs? Do you have your own lucky charm?

_____

_____

_____

_____

_____

_____

3. Why didn't Via tell her parents about the school play?

_____

_____

_____

_____

_____

_____

Character Word Cloud

Come up with at least ten personality traits for Justin, and find the textual evidence to support your answers. Then, use these traits to create a word cloud portraying this character, or you may include a picture, image, or symbol that you think can represent him.

Personal Traits	Textual Evidence
understanding / kind-hearted	Justin concealed his surprise and appeared calm when he saw Auggie for the first time. (p. 187)

13

Part Six: August
Pages 205–234

 Word Power

1. snitch *v.* 打小報告
2. gross *adj.* 噁心的
3. have a crush on sb 迷戀某人
4. cooties *n.* 蝨子
5. hearing aid *n.* 助聽器

6. audiology *n.* 聽力學
7. standing ovation *n.* 起立鼓掌
8. not a dry eye in the house
   在場的人都感動落淚

 Reading Comprehension

(　) 1. How did Auggie and Jack get back at Julian for writing mean notes?
　　　(A) They left sarcastic notes in Julian's locker.
　　　(B) They snitched on Julian.
　　　(C) They hired a "hit man" to hurt Julian.
　　　(D) They posted those mean notes on the bulletin board.

(　) 2. Which character in *Star Wars* does Auggie look like when he wears the
　　　hearing aids?
　　　(A) Wookiee.
　　　(B) Padawan.
　　　(C) Darth Sidious.
　　　(D) Lobot.

(　) 3. What is Auggie's cave made of?
　　　(A) Cushions.
　　　(B) Bricks.
　　　(C) Stuffed animals.
　　　(D) Stones.

Further Discussion

1. Why did Auggie compare himself to the North Pole at the science fair?

   _____

   _____

   _____

   _____

   _____

   _____

2. What does Auggie's mother think of heaven? What does heaven look like in your imagination?

   _____

   _____

   _____

   _____

   _____

   _____

3. Auggie thinks that everyone should get a standing ovation at least once in their lives. What is your view about standing ovations? Have you ever got one? Share the story with us.

   _____

   _____

   _____

   _____

   _____

   _____

Character Relationship Chart

Auggie's second part in the story begins with a quote from Shakespeare's famous tragedy—*Hamlet*. The following names are the main characters from *Hamlet*. Watch the videos online, and then try to find out their relationship by filling in their names in the chart.

🎬 How to Pronounce Character Names in Shakespeare's *Hamlet*

🎬 Shakespeare's *Hamlet* CliffsNotes Summary

Claudius	Gertrude	Horatio	Ghost of King Hamlet	Laertes
Ophelia	Polonius	Hamlet	Rosencrantz & Guildenstern	

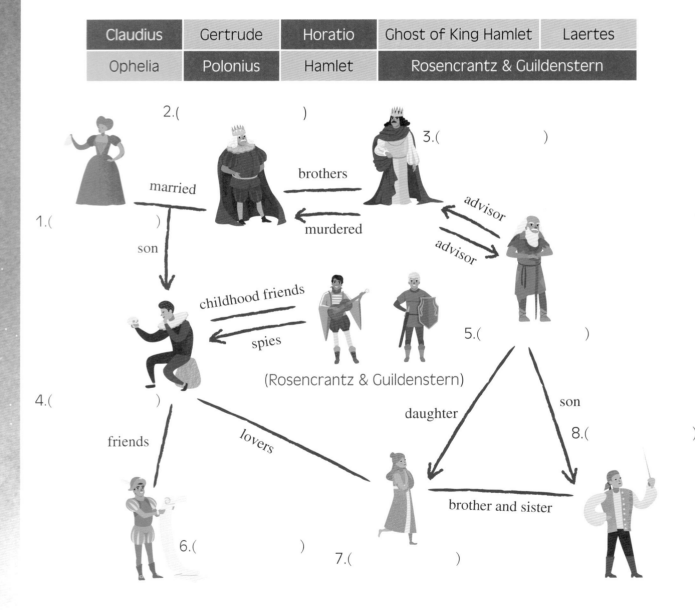

2.(   )

3.(   )

brothers

married

murdered

advisor

advisor

1.(   )

son

childhood friends

spies

(Rosencrantz & Guildenstern)

5.(   )

4.(   )

friends

lovers

daughter

son

8.(   )

brother and sister

6.(   )

7.(   )

42

Character Comparison

☐ SCAN ME

Have you ever seen the musical film *The Lion King*? Do you know *The Lion King* was inspired by *Hamlet*? Try to find out the similarities and differences between them. 🎬 *The Lion King* — Original Trailer

A. Identify the characters in *Hamlet* corresponding to those in *The Lion King* and fill in the blanks.

The Characters in *The Lion King*	
( ) 1. Simba	( ) 5. Nala
( ) 2. Mufasa	( ) 6. Zazu
( ) 3. Scar	( ) 7. Timon and Pumbaa
( ) 4. Sarabi	( ) 8. Hyenas
The Characters in *Hamlet*	
(A) Gertrude	(E) Polonius
(B) Laertes	(F) Hamlet
(C) Ghost of King Hamlet	(G) Claudius
(D) Horatio	(H) Ophelia

B. Compare and contrast the two following characters, and then complete the chart with their similarities and differences.

Simba vs. Hamlet	
Similarities	**Differences**

14

Part Seven: Miranda
Pages 235–248

Word Power

1. weirdo *n.* 怪胎
2. halter top *n.* 削肩背心
3. bounty hunter *n.* 賞金獵人
4. prude *n.* 老古板
5. xerox machine *n.* 影印機
6. last-minute jitters *n.* 上臺前的緊張
7. bittersweet *adj.* 苦甜參半的
8. euphoric *adj.* 異常興奮的

Reading Comprehension

(　) 1. Which of the following was **NOT** a lie Miranda told?
    (A) Her parents are in Europe.
    (B) She has a dog named Daisy.
    (C) She has a boyfriend named Justin.
    (D) She has a little brother who is deformed.

(　) 2. Which play does Mr. Davenport finally choose to put on?
    (A) *The Elephant Man*.
    (B) *The Lion, the Witch and the Wardrobe*.
    (C) *Our Town*.
    (D) *War and Peace*.

(　) 3. How does the Pullman family plan to celebrate after the show?
    (A) By having a late-night dinner.
    (B) By singing karaoke.
    (C) By going to the amusement park.
    (D) By attending David Bowie's memorial concert.

1. Even though Ella and Via were both Miranda's friends, there was a huge difference between them. What was it?

   _____

   _____

   _____

   _____

   _____

   _____

2. What play did the school originally plan on doing? Why did Miranda ask Mr. Davenport to switch the play?

   _____

   _____

   _____

   _____

   _____

   _____

   _____

3. What might be the reasons that Miranda pretended to be sick on opening night?

   _____

   _____

   _____

   _____

   _____

   _____

Problem and Solution

Let's explore the world of Miranda. Answer the following four questions to learn more about Miranda.

1. What do you know about Miranda?	2. What was Miranda's problem with Via?
3. What did Miranda change after going to the summer camp?	4. How did Miranda make up with Via?

15

Part Eight: August
Pages 249–270

Word Power

1. bunk bed *n.* 上下舖
2. rain poncho *n.* 雨衣
3. chop chop 快一點
4. goof off 鬼混

5. rec room *n.* 娛樂室
6. hopscotch *v.* 像玩跳房子遊戲那樣跳
7. hysterical *adj.* 歇斯底里的
8. stand sb's ground 某人拒不讓步

Reading Comprehension

(　) 1. What did Auggie and Christopher play during the sleepover?
　　 (A) A lightsaber duel.
　　 (B) Monopoly.
　　 (C) Legos *Star Wars*.
　　 (D) Hopscotch.

(　) 2. What is Baboo?
　　 (A) A stuffed animal.
　　 (B) A dog.
　　 (C) A duffel bag.
　　 (D) A character in *Star Wars*.

(　) 3. Which movie is shown on Big Movie Nights at Broarwood?
　　 (A) *The Sound of Music*.
　　 (B) *Beauty and the Beast*.
　　 (C) *Pac-Man: The Movie*.
　　 (D) *Star Wars: The Force Awakens*.

Further Discussion

1. Why was Auggie nervous about the nature retreat?

_____

_____

_____

_____

_____

_____

2. What was the significance of the class trip for Auggie's growth?

_____

_____

_____

_____

_____

_____

3. What kind of person do you think Amos is?

_____

_____

_____

_____

_____

_____

Journal Writing

What is the most unforgettable school trip in your life? Do you have a good memory of it like Auggie? Try to describe what happened during the trip and write a 150–200 word journal.

Date: _____

Location: _____

_____

_____

_____

_____

_____

_____

_____

_____

_____

_____

_____

_____

_____

_____

_____

_____

_____

16

Part Eight: August
Pages 271~288

Word Power

1. cotton candy *n.* 棉花糖
2. thug *n.* 惡棍
3. gulp down *v.* 大口飲下
4. tug-of-war *n.* 拔河
5. get picked on 被找碴
6. knuckle-punch *v.* 兄弟般的擊拳儀式
7. be out of the loop 不是圈內人
8. press charges 提出控告

Reading Comprehension

( ) 1. How did Isabel react when Auggie got off the bus?
 (A) She gave him a welcoming smile.
 (B) She waved at him.
 (C) She gave him a tight hug.
 (D) She asked him a lot of questions.

( ) 2. Who is Bear?
 (A) A new puppy in Auggie's family.
 (B) One of Auggie's stuffed animals.
 (C) A nickname for Amos.
 (D) The mascot of Beecher Prep.

( ) 3. What did Auggie draw in his Self-Portrait as an Animal?
 (A) A lamb.
 (B) A swan.
 (C) A bear.
 (D) A duck.

Further Discussion

1. Why did Isabel say "Sometimes people surprise us"?

_____

_____

_____

_____

_____

_____

2. Why did a big shift take place in Auggie's school when they went back to school after the nature retreat?

_____

_____

_____

_____

_____

_____

3. Read through pages 311 to 312. Among Mr. Browne's precepts, which one is your favorite? Why?

_____

_____

_____

_____

_____

_____

Portraits as Animals

Auggie drew himself as a duck for the New Year Art Show because he thought he looked like a duck. What animal would you choose to represent yourself, your family, your teacher, or your best friend? Please draw them below and state your reasons.

Myself:

Reason:

_____:

Reason:

_____:

Reason:

_____:

Reason:

17

Part Eight: August
Pages 289–310

Word Power

1. gel *n.* 髮膠
2. ignition *n.* 引擎點火
3. opening remarks *n.* 開幕詞
4. commencement address *n.* 結業致詞
5. roll call *n.* 點名
6. verbosity *n.* 廢話
7. zone out 走神
8. exemplary *adj.* 可作楷模的

Reading Comprehension

(　　) 1. Who threw out Auggie's astronaut helmet?
    (A) Nate.
    (B) Isabel.
    (C) Via.
    (D) Miranda.

(　　) 2. How were the seats arranged at the awards presentation?
    (A) According to the students' height.
    (B) According to the students' number.
    (C) According to the students' academic performance.
    (D) In alphabetical order by the students' last names.

(　　) 3. What kind of gold medal did Summer win?
    (A) Overall academic performance.
    (B) Sports.
    (C) Creative writing.
    (D) Music.

Further Discussion

1. How does Mr. Tushman measure success? How about you?

_____
_____
_____
_____
_____
_____
_____

2. Why did Auggie receive the Henry Ward Beecher medal? Give examples from the novel how Auggie exhibited his courage, kindness, or friendship.

_____
_____
_____
_____
_____
_____
_____

3. What did Auggie's mother whisper in his ear at the end of this chapter? What do her words mean to you?

_____
_____
_____
_____
_____
_____

Awards Presentation Planning

Imagine you are one of the organizers of
the awards presentation at Beecher Prep.
How would you plan this memorable event?
Try to answer the following questions.

1. What theme would you choose? What activities would you integrate to
   amaze or entertain your audience?

   _____
   _____
   _____
   _____
   _____
   _____

2. Come up with three creative or interesting award titles and write down at
   least two possible nominees for each award in Auggie's class.

   _____
   _____
   _____

3. Try to pick out the winner for each award and explain why you gave the
   award to him/her.

   _____
   _____
   _____
   _____
   _____
   _____

18

Overall Review

Congratulations on finishing *Wonder*. Now imagine you are a renowned book critic, and your fans are waiting for your review of this book.

My Rating:

1. Introduce the book briefly. What are the themes in the book?

_____

_____

_____

_____

_____

_____

2. Whose point of view is missing in the book? Why do you think R. J. Palacio made such an arrangement?

_____

_____

_____

_____

_____

_____

3. What is your favorite part in the book?

_____

_____

_____

_____

_____

_____

4. Choose one sentence or scene that resonates with you and explain why.

_____

_____

_____

_____

_____

_____

5. Who would you like to recommend this book to? For example, you can say, "If you like. . ., you will love this book," or "I would recommend this book to anyone who likes. . . ."

_____

_____

_____

_____

_____

_____

◆ Harry Potter and the Sorcerer's Stone
解讀攻略

戴逸群 主編／簡嘉妤 編著／ Ian Fletcher 審閱

Lexile 藍思分級：880

☞ 議題：品德教育、家庭教育、多元文化、閱讀素養

◆ Love, Simon 解讀攻略

戴逸群 主編／林冠瑋 編著／ Ian Fletcher 審閱

Lexile 藍思分級：640

☞ 議題：性別平等、人權教育、多元文化、閱讀素養

◆ Matilda 解讀攻略

戴逸群 主編／林佳紋 編著／ Joseph E. Schier 審閱

Lexile 藍思分級：840

☞ 議題：性別平等、人權教育、家庭教育、閱讀素養

Answer Key

Lesson 1
Reading Comprehension
1. (B)   2. (A)   3. (D)

Lesson 2
Reading Comprehension
1. (C)   2. (B)   3. (B)

Lesson 3
Reading Comprehension
1. (C)   2. (A)   3. (C)

Lesson 4
Reading Comprehension
1. (C)   2. (B)   3. (D)

Lesson 5
Reading Comprehension
1. (D)   2. (D)   3. (C)

Lesson 6
Reading Comprehension
1. (C)   2. (B)   3. (D)

Lesson 7
Reading Comprehension
1. (C)   2. (A)   3. (B)

Lesson 8
Reading Comprehension
1. (A)   2. (A)   3. (C)

Lesson 9
Reading Comprehension
1. (A)   2. (C)   3. (C)

Lesson 10
Reading Comprehension
1. (A)   2. (B)   3. (B)

Lesson 11
Reading Comprehension
1. (C)   2. (C)   3. (B)

Lesson 12
Reading Comprehension
1. (B)   2. (C)   3. (A)

Lesson 13
Reading Comprehension
1. (A)   2. (D)   3. (C)

Character Relationship Chart
1. Gertrude   2. Ghost of King Hamlet
3. Claudius   4. Hamlet
5. Polonius   6. Horatio
7. Ophelia   8. Laertes

Character Comparison
1. (F)   2. (C)   3.(G)   4. (A)
5. (H)   6. (E)   7.(D)   8. (B)

Lesson 14
Reading Comprehension
1. (C)   2. (C)   3. (A)

Lesson 15
Reading Comprehension
1. (C)   2. (A)   3. (A)

Lesson 16
Reading Comprehension
1. (C)   2. (A)   3. (D)

Lesson 17
Reading Comprehension
1. (A)   2. (D)   3. (C)

打造英文小說的「閱讀素養」課程

解開文本迷津、讀出深度思考力、攻克閱讀英文長篇小說的完全攻略

從讀到寫逐步搭建鷹架，長篇閱讀 SO EASY！

依據校園生活及人生課題精選一系列青少年英文小說，從文本延伸設計多元有趣的英文學習活動，逐步為英文閱讀歷程搭好鷹架，充分領略閱讀英文小說的樂趣。

單字學習、閱讀理解、批判思考，輕鬆 GET！

Word Power 精選重要且貼近生活的實用單字，活用不死記，擴增英文單字庫；Reading Comprehension 引導讀者擷取訊息、推敲文意，協助理解該閱讀範圍；Further Discussion 培養語文表達以及思辨能力。

整合資訊、獨立思考、解決問題，素養力 UP！

結合社群網站、日記或書信等生活化題材，設計學思並進的創意解讀活動，讀出深度思考力與表達力，學習從不同角度用英文解決問題，培養接軌國際的英文素養力。

班級：_____

座號：_____

姓名：_____

藍思分級	議題
790	品德教育、生命教育家庭教育、閱讀素養

原文小說適用版本：Wonder（9781524764463）

ISBN 978-957-14-6809-9　　(805)

NTD 200

9 789571 468099

870460

三民網路書店
www.sanmin.com.tw

英文小説解讀攻略

奇幻篇

戴逸群 —— 主編

簡嘉妤 —— 編著

Ian Fletcher —— 審閱

三民書局